CHRISTMAS
MORNING

by Cheryl Ryan

Illustrated by Jenny Mattheson

SCHOLASTIC INC.

New York   Toronto   London   Auckland   Sydney
Mexico City   New Delhi   Hong Kong   Buenos Aires

For Sarah

—C.R.

For all the folks at Christmas Camp

—J.M.

Text copyright © 2004 by Cheryl Ryan.
Illustrations copyright © 2004 by Jenny Mattheson.
All rights reserved. Published by Scholastic Inc. SCHOLASTIC, CARTWHEEL BOOKS,
and associated logos are trademarks and/or registered trademarks of Scholastic Inc.

Library of Congress Cataloging-in-Publication Data

Ryan, Cheryl.
Christmas morning / by Cheryl Ryan; illustrated by Jenny Mattheson.
p. cm.
Summary: Cumulative rhyme featuring traditions of Christmas, including snow, St. Nick, and a nutcracker.
ISBN 0-439-41425-3 (Paper Over Board)
[1. Christmas--Fiction. 2. Stories in rhyme.] I. Mattheson, Jenny, ill. II. Title.
PZ8.3.H245Th 2004
[E]--dc22   2003024114
10 9 8 7 6 5 4 3 2 1   04 05 06 07 08
Printed in Singapore 46
First printing, October 2004

This is the house where the children slept.

This is the snow
that fell on the house
where the children slept.

This is the sleigh
that flew through the snow
that fell on the house
where the children slept.

These are the reindeer
who pulled the sleigh
that flew through the snow
that fell on the house
where the children slept.

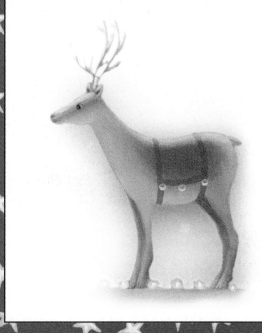

These are the reins
covered with bells
that guided the reindeer
who pulled the sleigh
that flew through the snow
that fell on the house
where the children slept.

And this is Saint Nick
who snapped the reins
covered with bells
that guided the reindeer
who pulled the sleigh
that flew through the snow
that fell on the house
where the children slept.

This is the sack filled with toys

flung over the back

of old Saint Nick

who snapped the reins

covered with bells

that guided the reindeer

who pulled the sleigh

that flew through the snow

that fell on the house

where the children slept.

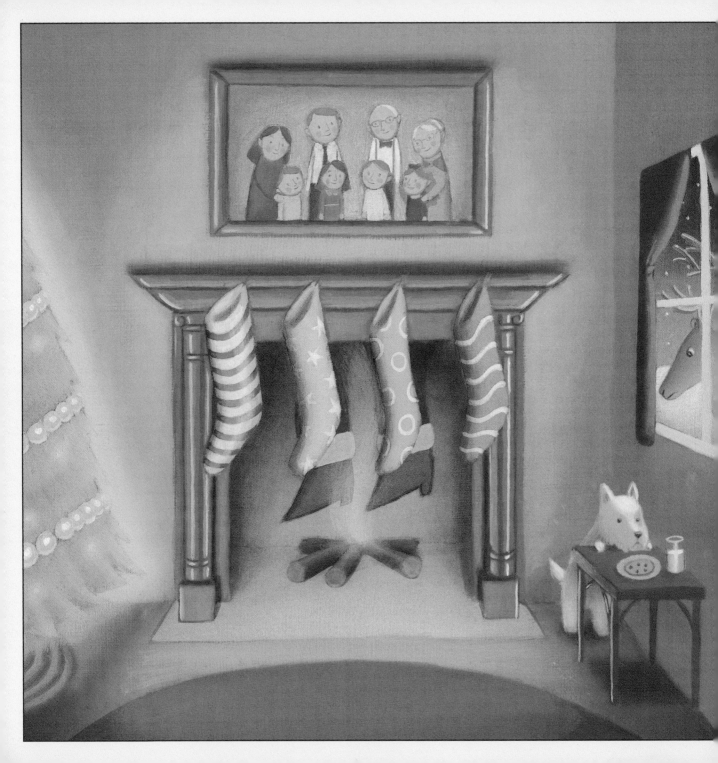

These are the stockings

waiting for toys

to come from the sack

flung over the back

of old Saint Nick

who snapped the reins

covered with bells

that guided the reindeer

who pulled the sleigh

that flew through the snow

that fell on the house

where the children slept.

This is the box

in one of the socks

filled with toys

that came from the sack

flung over the back

of old Saint Nick

who snapped the reins

covered with bells

that guided the reindeer

who pulled the sleigh

that flew through the snow

that fell on the house

where the children slept.

This is the doll

in the box

in one of the socks

filled with toys

that came from the sack

flung over the back

of old Saint Nick

who snapped the reins

covered with bells

that guided the reindeer

who pulled the sleigh

that flew through the snow

that fell on the house

where the children slept.

This is the Rat King

and all of his pack

who frightened the doll

in the box

in one of the socks

filled with toys

that came from the sack

flung over the back

of old Saint Nick

who snapped the reins

covered with bells

that guided the reindeer

who pulled the sleigh

that flew through the snow

that fell on the house

where the children slept.

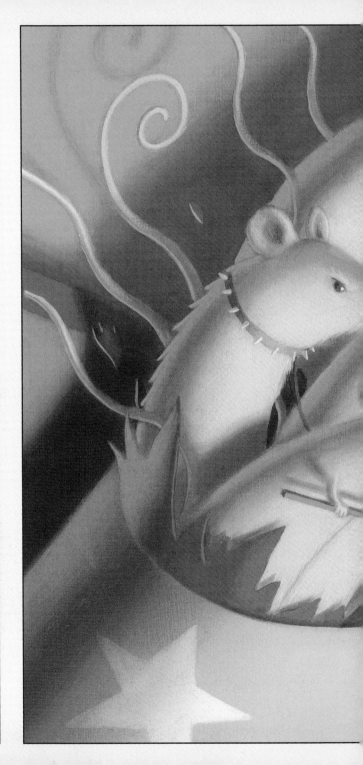

This is the Nutcracker
who fought the Rat
and all of his pack
who frightened the doll
in the box
in one of the socks
filled with toys
that came from the sack
flung over the back
of old Saint Nick
who snapped the reins
covered with bells
that guided the reindeer
who pulled the sleigh
that flew through the snow
that fell on the house
where the children slept.

This is the train on the track
that carried the Nutcracker
forward and back
to fight the Rat
and all of his pack
who frightened the doll
in the box
in one of the socks
filled with toys
that came from the sack
flung over the back
of old Saint Nick
who snapped the reins
covered with bells
that guided the reindeer
who pulled the sleigh
that flew through the snow
that fell on the house
where the children slept.

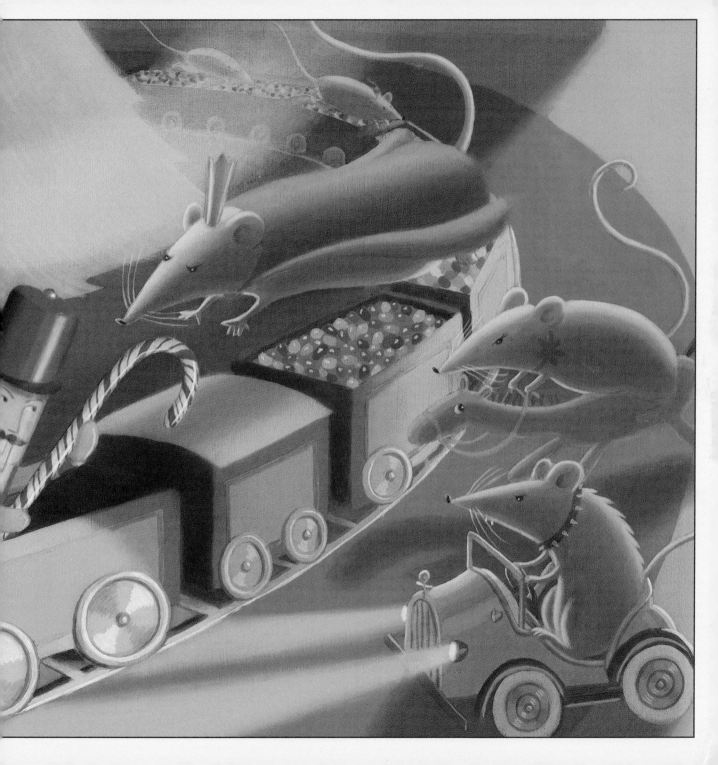

These are the children
who wake to find
the train on the track
that carried the Nutcracker
forward and back
to fight the Rat
and all of his pack
who frightened the doll
in the box
in one of the socks
filled with toys

that came from the sack

flung over the back

of old Saint Nick

who snapped the reins

covered with bells

that guided the reindeer

who pulled the sleigh

that flew through the snow

that fell on the house

where the children slept.

And this is Chr

stmas morning!

MOTIONS TO ACCOMPANY THE STORY

HOUSE
Hands over head in an inverted "V."

SNOW
Hands over head, wave fingers lightly as arms are lowered.

SLEIGH
Hands, palms together, weave from left to right.

REINDEER
Hands on either side of the head, thumbs touching head above each ear.

REINS
Close hands as if holding reins, shake wrists.

SAINT NICK
Pat stomach with both hands and say, "HO! HO! HO!"

SACK
Both hands together over right shoulder as if carrying a sack.

STOCKINGS
Hand hangs invisible stocking on an invisible nail.

BOX
Show dimensions, length and width, with both hands.

DOLL
Hands together at side of head, head tilted, bat eyes adoringly.

RAT KING
Hold hands out like claws, snarl, and show teeth.

NUTCRACKER
Give a salute!

TRAIN
Hand pulls whistle cord, shout, "WHOOO! WHOOO!"

CHILDREN
Shout, "HOORAY!"